SNOWIE ROLIE

W9-BNV-492

SNOWIE ROLIE

by
William
Joyce

SCHOLASTIC INC.

New York Toronto London Auckland Sydney
Mexico City New Delhi Hong Kong Buenos Aires

Rolie Polie Olie lived in a
land where it never snowed.
He often wished for the wonders
a snowy day could bring.

Then one bright morning, the sun that shone on Olie's world blew a bulb . . .

and it started to snow!

As the world
grew white all around,
Olie and Zowie began
to build a friend . . .

named Mr. Snowie!

Oh,
what
fun
it
with
was
Snowie
to
on
ride
their
sleigh!

But the sun got a brand-new bulb, so the world
became warm and the snow became melty.

What to do? What to do? They had
a friend they couldn't keep cool!

So they took a worthy
risk and rocketed to
Chillsville with the
A/C on full blast.

The snowcapped mountains showed them the way.

But the North wind
tried to eat them up.

And down they
crashed . . .

to a place they'd heard of only in stories.

"Welcome to Chillsville," said Klanky Klaus.
"You must be hungry from your travels."

They feasted on snowdrop soup, icicle cake, and sky-high snowball pie.

And after that, they danced a chilly cha cha . . .

all the way to Mr. Snowie's
cool new house.

"We'll miss you, Mr. Snowie," said Zowie.
"But you'll be safe from now on," said Olie.

It was oh so hard
to say good-bye.

"**W**e wished for snow and we got a new friend," said Olie. "I wish we could stay together," sighed Zowie as they rocketed away.

The journey home
was swift and sure.
Soon sleep came,
and snowy dreams
helped smiles return.

By morning, the snow was almost gone, and where Snowie once stood, there was a present . . .

a happy reminder
of their faraway friend.

Happy, sad, and everything in between—
what wonders a single snowy day can bring!

Super-special thanks
to the hardest-working man
in Robot Land, Jordan Thistlewood.
Also thanks to Susie Grondin, Shannon
Gilley, Gavin Boyle, Ian MacLeod, and
Ms. Lehn, the El Pammo Supreme-o, and the
Nelvana 3D production group for the reuse
of their models. And finally, thanks to
Alicia Mikles and Ruiko Tokunaga,
twin Valkyries of Pixelation.

For my
faraway
friends
—WJ

No part of
this publication may be reproduced in
whole or in part, or stored in a retrieval system,
or transmitted in any form or by any means, electronic, mechanical,
photocopying, recording, or otherwise, without written
permission of the publisher. For information regarding
permission, write to Laura Geringer Books, an imprint of HarperCollins
Publishers, 10 East 53rd Street, New York, NY 10022.

ISBN 0-439-35584-2

Copyright © 2000 by William Joyce.
All rights reserved.
Published by Scholastic Inc., 555 Broadway, New York, NY 10012,
by arrangement with Laura Geringer Books, an imprint of HarperCollins Publishers.
SCHOLASTIC and associated logos are trademarks and/or
registered trademarks of Scholastic Inc.

12 11 10 9 8 7 6 5   3 4 5 6/0

Printed in the U.S.A.   40

First Scholastic printing, November 2001

Typography by Alicia Mikles